D1288649

A NEED FOR SPEED!

Illustrated by Omar Hechtenkopf

A GOLDEN BOOK • NEW YORK

ISBN 978-0-553-53890-8
randomhousekids.com
MANUFACTURED IN CHINA
10 9 8 7 6 5

Blaze is the fastest Monster Machine around!

AJ is Blaze's driver and best friend.

Circle the two pictures of Blaze that match.

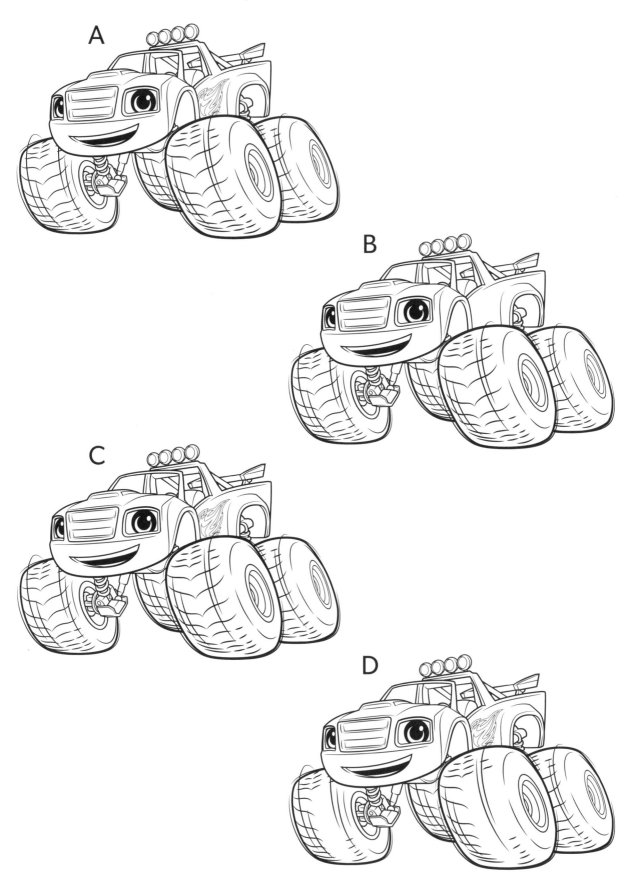

A

B

C

D

The Monster Dome is where all the big races and events take place.

Help Blaze and AJ get to the Monster Dome for the Monster Machine World Championship.

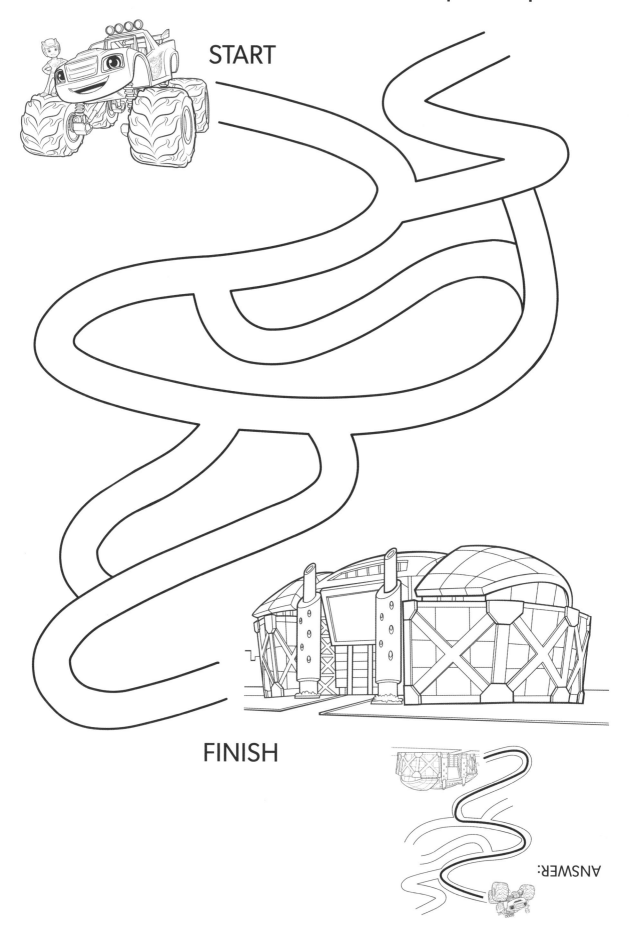

START

FINISH

ANSWER:

Gabby is the mechanic for the Monster Machines.

Gabby takes Blaze and AJ to meet
the Monster Machine racers.

Connect the dots to make a toolbox for Gabby.

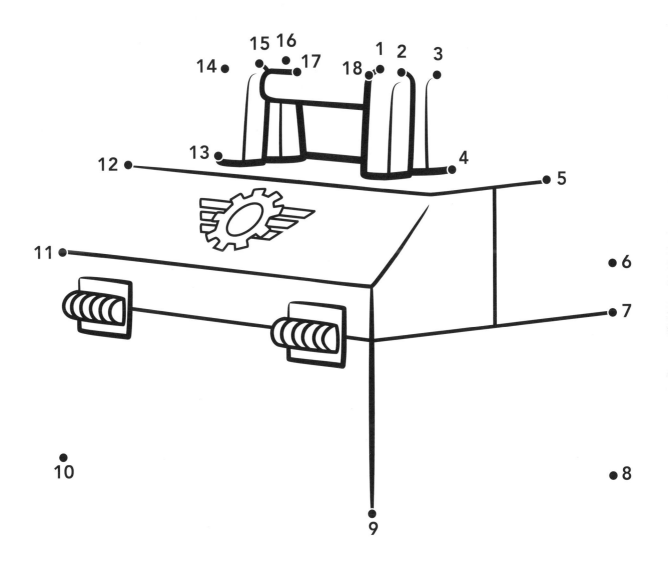

Stripes the tiger truck is always ready for action.

Zeg the dinosaur truck loves to smash and bash!

Starla is a hootin', hollerin' cowgirl Monster Machine!

Darington is a stunt truck who loves doing tricks.

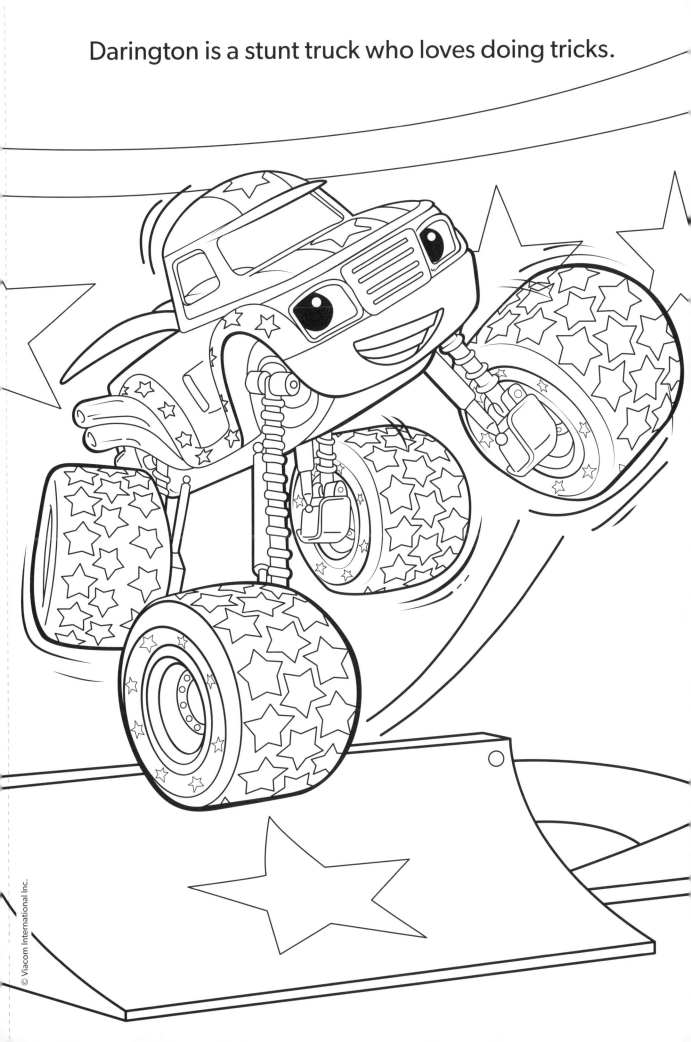

Crusher thinks he's the best racer ever. He will do anything to win—even cheat.

Pickle is a little truck with a big heart.

Match each Monster Machine with its close-up.

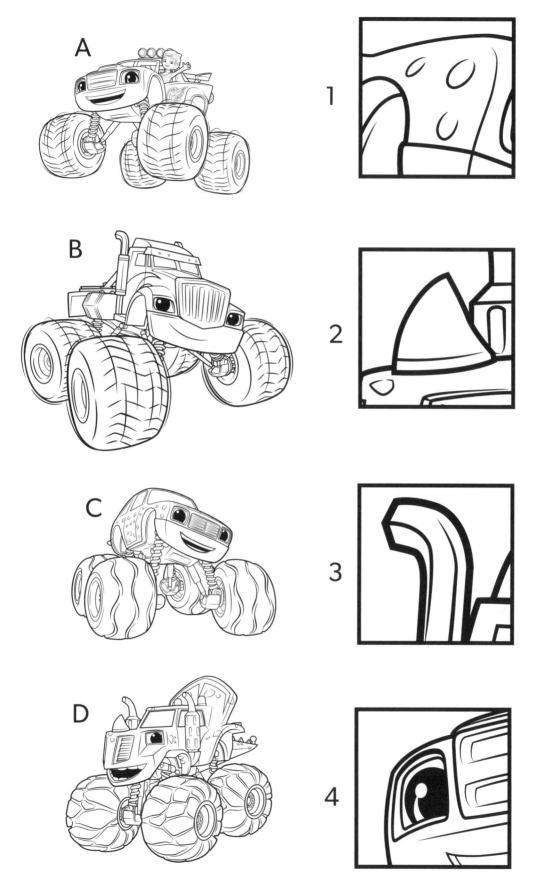

ANSWER: A-4, B-3, C-1, D-2.

STRIPES  **DARINGTON**  **CRUSHER** **STRIPES**

Crusher wants to be the only truck in the race so he can win. He blows bubbles with his Trouble Bubble Wand.

The bubbles pick up the Monster Machines
and carry them away!

Lug nuts! Blaze and AJ are trapped in a bubble!

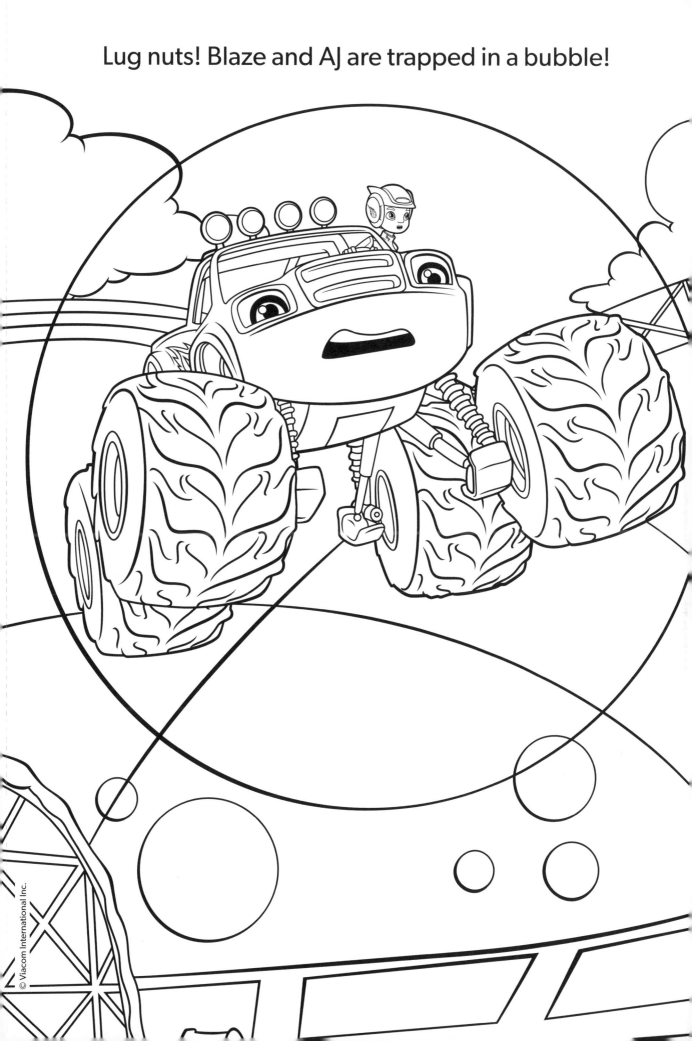

The bubble pops!

Blaze and AJ land in the Badlands.

They see Stripes hanging off a cliff!

Blaze jumps and saves Stripes with a bump
on the tires.

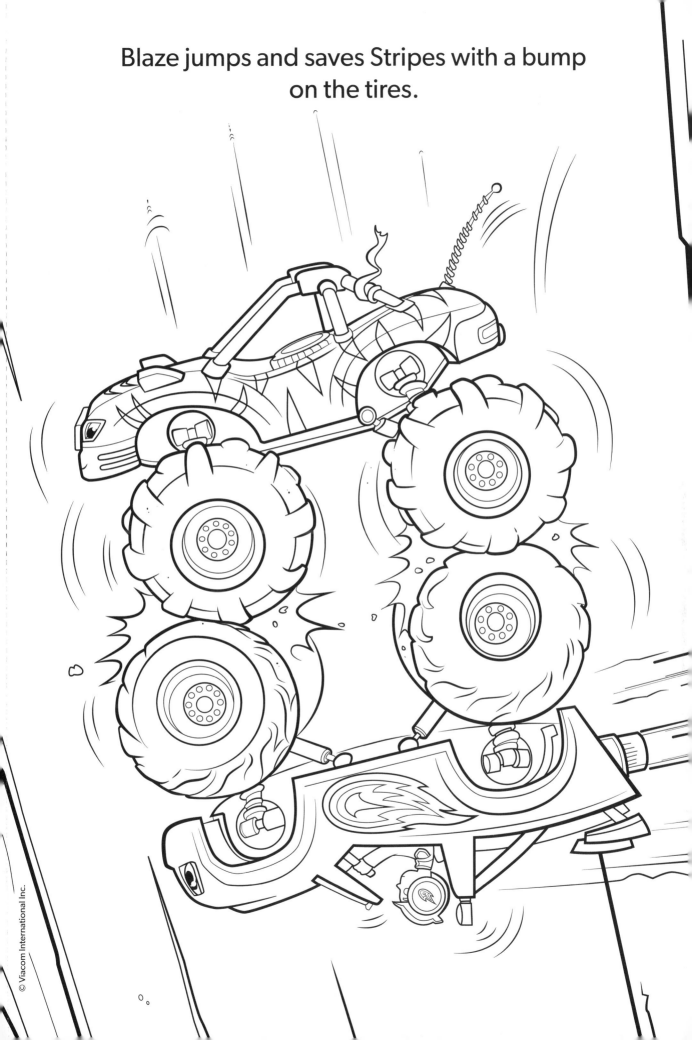

Blaze and Stripes zoom back to the Monster Dome before the race starts.

In the forest, Stripes picks up the scent of another Monster Machine.

It's Darington!

Darington is hiding from some Grizzly Trucks.

Find the Grizzly Truck who is different.

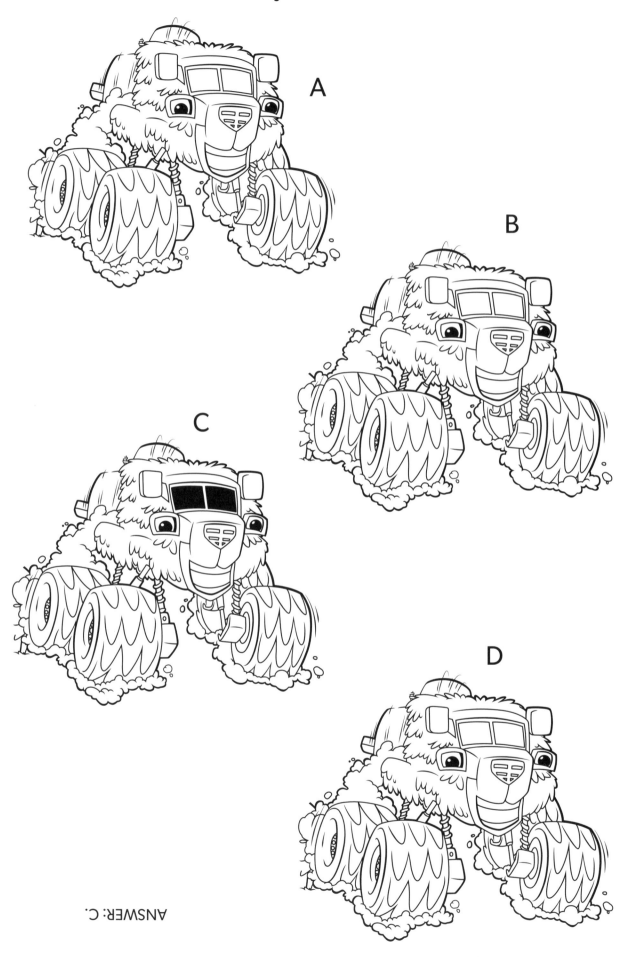

A

B

C

D

The Monster Machines need to speed away!

Uh-oh—a river! The Monster Machines have to cross it to escape the Grizzly Trucks.

Stripes finds a big, flat piece of wood.

Darington finds a big rock.

Blaze finds a curved piece of wood.

The flat piece of wood and the rock sink,
but the curved piece of wood has tall sides
to keep the water out!

Safe and dry, everyone floats across.

Back at the Monster Dome, the crowd cheers!

Crusher doesn't want the other racers to come back.
He builds another device to cheat with.

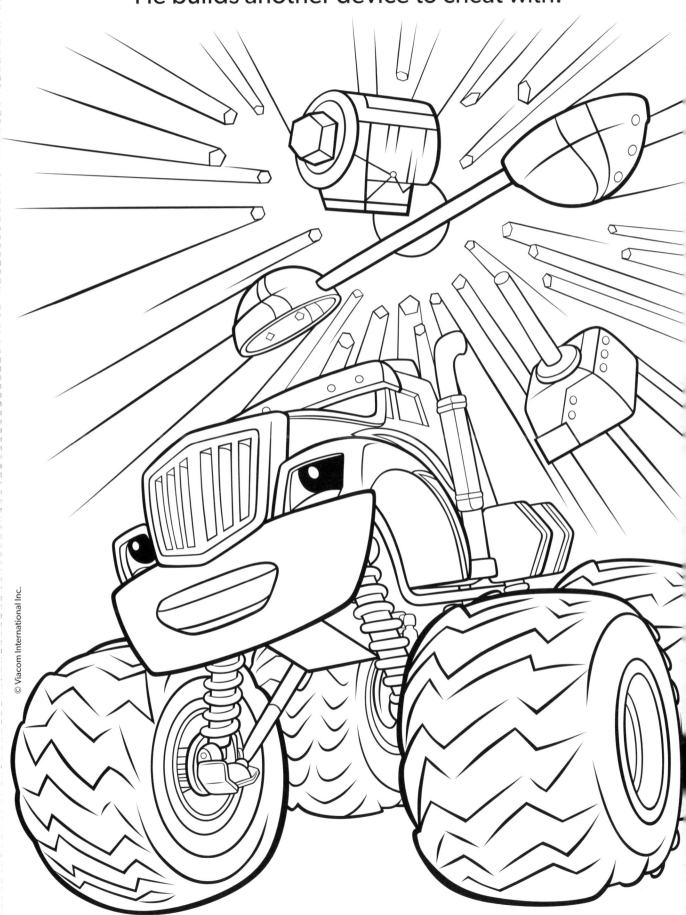

It's a Mechanical Mudslinger!

The Mechanical Mudslinger flings mud balls
at the Monster Machines!

AJ has an idea. With a hose, a nozzle,
and a spring-loaded arm, Blaze transforms into a . . .

. . . water-shooting Monster Machine!

Blaze blasts the mud balls!

Take that, Mechanical Mudslinger!

On their way back to the Monster Dome, Blaze and AJ see Zeg rolling down a mountain toward a cliff! Help them get to Zeg in time!

START

FINISH

ANSWER:

Blaze to the rescue!

The Monster Machines have to go through a cave.
But the entrance is too small!

ZEEEGGGG!

In the cave, they find Starla stuck at the bottom of a hole!

The Monster Machines use a pulley to get her out!

The Monster Machines race back
to the Monster Dome together.

Crusher has one trick up his tire—
Robot Knights!

The Robot Knights get power from their shields.

Blaze and AJ use a magnet to take away
the Robot Knights' shields—and their power!

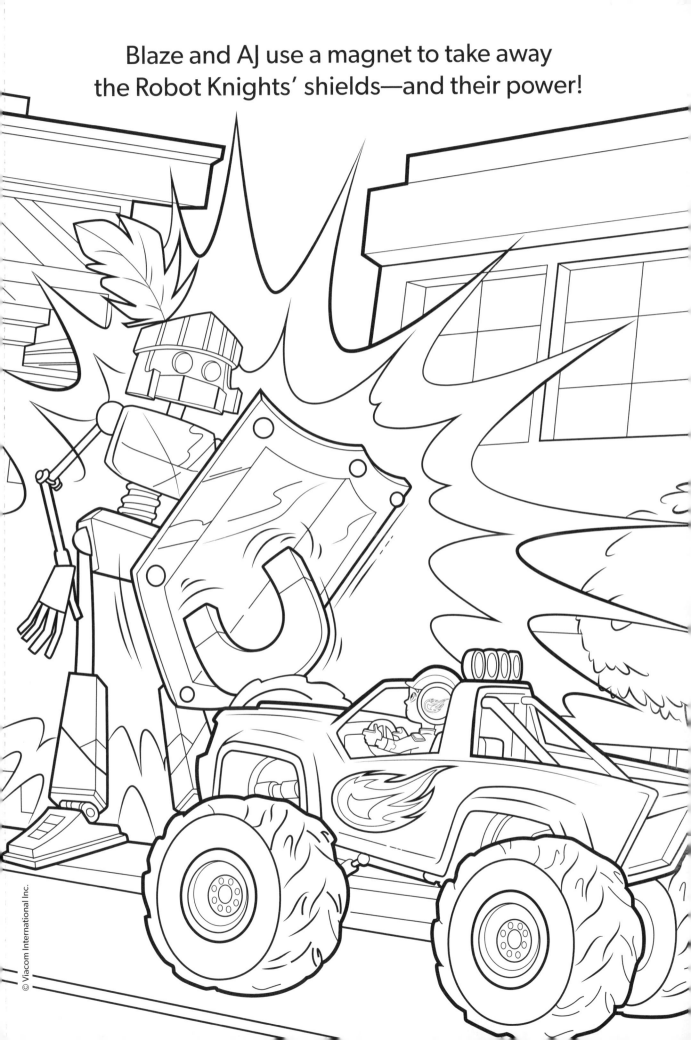

The championship race is about to start!
The Monster Machines ask Blaze
to race, too!

On your marks, get set, GO!

Crusher takes the lead.

Crusher has more dirty tricks!

Tire trouble!

Crusher's cheating ways are working!

Now it's just Blaze and Crusher.

Using Blazing Speed, Blaze zooms past Crusher!

When Blaze's spoiler goes up and his boosters
pop out, he can move at Blazing Speed!

Let's *blaaaze!*

The winner of the Monster Machine
World Championship is . . . Blaze!

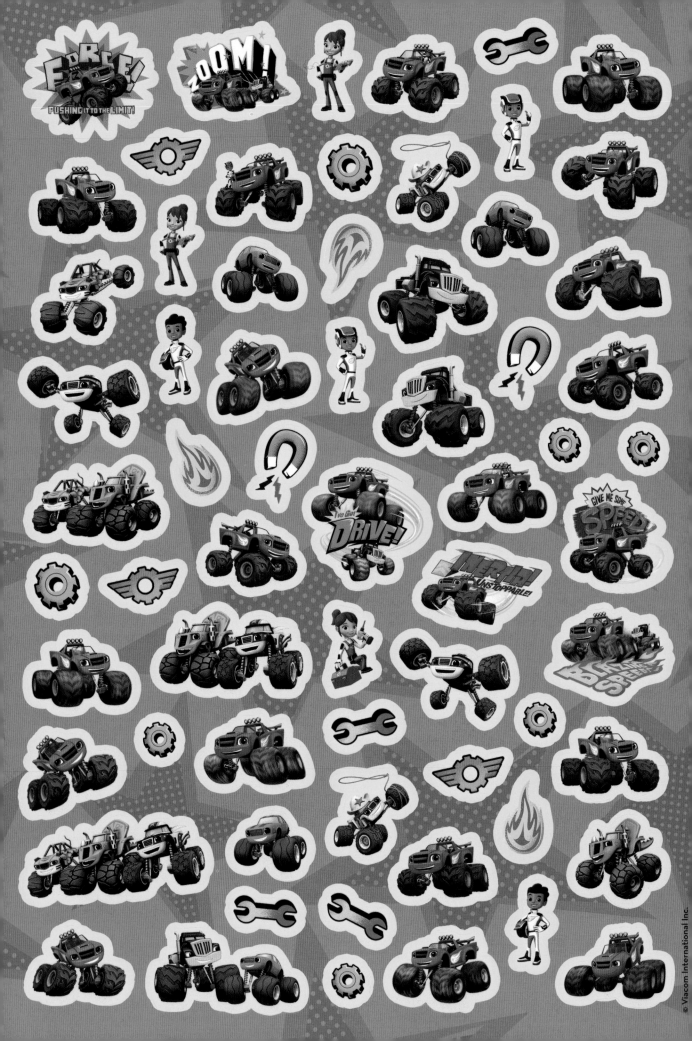

ONE TRICKY
TRUCK!
BLAZING SPEED!
Ready to Roll!
VROOOOM!!
Speed
BLAZING SPEED!
Speed
REV UP
AND
ROLL OUT!